Praise for *Otto and the Secret Light of Christmas*

'A gorgeous and unique collection of stories from Finland which deserve
a place in any holiday story collection ... Otto and his friends are brought to life
in sensitive, detailed illustrations on every page ... Perfect for bedtime reading
and an enduringly popular addition.'
–*Midwest Book Review*

'Complex sentence structures, rich vocabulary, and excellent dramatic pacing ...
Full-color illustrations in a soft-focus, mysterious style are interspersed throughout
the story ... An intriguing read-aloud for younger children and
an entertaining choice for independent readers.'
– *Kirkus Reviews*

'Finnish culture and traditions woven into the story make for a fresh take
on Christmas that can be read each day as the holiday approaches.'
– *School Library Journal*

'The illustrations are beyond marvelous ... This is a perfect holiday story.'
– *Youth Services Book Review* (starred review)

'The illustrations were beautiful ... I was eager to see what Otto would find out,
and you should read it, too.'
– *Kids Book Buzz*

'A magical Christmas story to share with children of all ages ... you can almost
feel the snow crunching under your shoes.'
– *The Reading Castle*

'Thoughtful, detailed illustrations on almost every page make this story
an ideal read for the child who wants to settle in a corner with a captivating book.'
– *Carousel*

'...a beautiful Christmas tale that is rich in references to Finnish folklore
and culture, and the soft, intricate, glowing illustrations added so much to my
appreciation of the story ... I can imagine parents and children cuddled up, drinking
hot chocolate and reading this book together over the Christmas holidays.'
– *Oregon Coast Youth Book Review*

Otto
and the Secret Light
the
of Christmas

Written by Nora Surojegin

Illustrated by Pirkko-Liisa Surojegin

Translated by Jill G. Timbers

Floris
Books

First published in Finnish in 2010 as *Untu ja sydäntalven salaisuus*
by Kustannusosakeyhtiö Otava, Helsinki
This edition published in 2016 by Floris Books
Text © 2010 Nora Surojegin and Kustannusosakeyhtiö Otava
Illustrations © 2010 Pirkko-Liisa Surojegin and
Kustannusosakeyhtiö Otava
English version © 2016 Floris Books
Second printing 2018

British Library CIP Data available
ISBN 978-178250-323-1
Printed in Malaysia

Contents

 1. New Winds   9
 2. The Apple Thief   14
 3. Kekri, King of the Forest   20
 4. A Humming Glow Worm   27
 5. The Mupples and the Hazytales   35
 6. An Evening Underground   44
 7. The Leaf Fairies' Last Dance   51
 8. Frosted Bear   56
 9. The Secret of the Snow Lonttis   62
10. Booming Burl   69
11. Little Hiss   76
12. Ironworm   82
13. A Chatty Reindeer   91
14. Fires in the Sky   96

1. New Winds

Seagull Schooner glided high up above the coastline, which wiggled cheerfully as the waves swelled and receded. Late summer winds danced among wisps of cloud, and the morning sun glittered on the sea below.

Autumn often brought new adventures, and today Schooner detected a strong scent of change in the air: a feeling of something new and exciting.

He curved softly above the grey rocks towards a small, lichen-covered log hut below where the rocks met the sea. A tiny lantern swung at its door.

Schooner landed and stretched his wings. He had lost a leg in an accident long ago, so his movement on land was slow. Hopping, he circled the hut, and soon spotted his friend Otto among the rocks on the beach. Schooner had known Otto for years. They had both travelled the seas and been toughened by the northern winds. They were both very calm, and a deep friendship had grown between them.

Otto wore a leather hat with a hem that flapped in the sea breeze and two horns that expressed his mood, like the ears of a dog. His moss-green tunic was decorated with ancient designs that told tales of his ancestors, and around his waist he carried a small knife and an amulet to protect him from danger. Between his grey beard and eyebrows, his eyes sparkled like fish in the sun.

Otto was piling up white stones on the beach as a marker for passing ships, and humming merrily as he worked.

"Greetings, old friend!" said Schooner.

"Greetings!" Otto replied heartily. "How good it is to see you again!"

Otto spent a lot of time thinking and he was tired of storing his thoughts in his head. Now, with his good friend for company, he began to put them into words without really considering how they would pop out of his mouth.

"What if my roof were to collapse?" Otto began. Ignoring Schooner's astonishment, he continued, "If it collapsed when I was in the hut and flattened me to the size of a mouse dropping, would I lie there, squashed, and think to myself, *I've had a bright and colourful life?*"

"Where on earth did that thought come from?" Schooner marvelled.

Otto dug a battered postcard from his coat pocket, showing a sparkling star-filled sky. Beneath the picture, decorative letters proclaimed:

THE LIGHT OF CHRISTMAS!

Fingering the crumpled edges, Otto sighed. "I found this on the beach, washed up by the sea. On the back someone has written a message:

Wishing you light in the midst of winter,
and a joy-filled Christmas season.

"I've been wondering what Christmas might be. I've never seen it."

Winter on the coast of Finland was dark and dismal. If this 'Christmas' could brighten it, Otto felt he might like to find it and maybe bring some back.

Schooner studied his friend. "I have often heard tales of strange customs in the far north," he said, "and rumours of something that gives more light than ten lanterns. Maybe that's where Christmas can be found."

After Schooner left, Otto sat on the dock, thinking. Over the years he had survived terrible storms and battled ferocious monsters, but he had never felt this nervous. He had butterflies in his stomach. Light in the winter's darkness, now *that* was definitely worth investigating. Otto didn't want to find himself flattened under his own roof thinking he might have missed the greatest adventure of his life!

As dusk fell, he rose, swept out the entrance to his hut and stepped inside. Looking at it through new eyes, Otto thought his cosy home suddenly seemed cold and small.

He could feel two piercing eyes staring at him from the corner of the room. It was Little Grump, who shared Otto's hut.

"What does that old gull want now?" Little Grump snapped.

Otto looked at his tiny companion with disgust. "I'd ask you not to speak that way," he said. "Schooner is my good friend."

"Whatever," Little Grump sniffed, and he started sweeping the entrance to his hole in the corner of the room with a spruce branch. Little Grump was often mean, but he could also be very kind. "As long as he doesn't put crazy ideas into your head," he snapped. "Lights in the far north... Everyone knows there's nothing up north except dark woods and reindeer crunching around on ice. Who'd want to go there?!"

"I've never seen a reindeer either," Otto said.

"What's to see? They're just stupid little moose with small heads," Little Grump snorted.

Otto humphed in reply and sank back into his own thoughts. He watched the candlelight throwing shadows on the walls and thought very hard. So what if he did find only small stupid reindeer? Before he drifted off to sleep, Otto resolved to set off at daybreak in search of Christmas, the secret light of the north.

The sun was already high in the sky the next morning when Little Grump emerged from his cubbyhole, stretching, and craving blueberry tea. Glancing over at the hut's doorway, he noticed that Otto's warm tunic and backpack were gone. On the floor lay the key to the pantry and a short note, explaining that Otto had gone away for a while and that he was leaving Little Grump all his fishtails and lingonberry pastries. Little Grump sat at the window, contentedly munching a pastry and looking at the bare rocky shore. For just a fleeting moment, he felt a pang of worry.

2. The Apple Thief

From a distance, one forest looks much like another. But treading slowly along the small paths, you notice that they can be very different. In some forests you can see far, and in others adventure may lurk behind the next bush.

Otto had been travelling through the dense forest towards the sunrise for some time and had already stopped for several snack breaks. Leaving the warm sea breezes of the coast behind, he noticed that autumn had sped forward here. As he plucked plump lingonberries and admired the glorious yellow of the birch trees, he felt carefree and happy. He made up a little song to speed along his journey:

> *Through berry grounds sweet,*
> *Past the pine trees' feet,*
> *Merrily onwards I go!*

It was peaceful in the forest. Many birds had already flown south, and the alders and spruce trees provided shelter from the wind. Otto followed paths among the trees as the sun winked through the branches. He continued his song as he headed towards a small clearing surrounded by large, moss-covered rocks. The sky was starting to get dark.

Otto heard a snuffling and grunting noise. He could see broken twigs and paw prints around a small sandy mound, but he couldn't see anyone. Then the snuffling grew louder, and the grasses swished back and forth, until suddenly a furry grey bottom

came into view. It turned to reveal a creature, which jumped when it saw Otto. Its black-and-white striped face was framed by small ears, and it looked as if its tiny brain was scrambling to come up with something to say. The creature looked a little guilty – possibly because its arms were full of apples.

"I'm not… I'm just…" the creature stammered. "The apples were lying there, doing nothing, so I thought I could take a few… I didn't expect someone to come after them!"

Otto gaped at the creature, which was tossing the apples into a hole on the other side of the mound.

"What are you talking about? I'm Otto. I'm seeking the light of the north."

The creature studied him for a moment, trying to decide whether the little grey man could be telling the truth or whether he was after the apples.

"The name's Badger," he said, introducing himself. "Coincidentally, I'm also a badger. My parents had a strange sense of humour. What kind of light are you seeking?"

"Have you ever heard of Christmas? It's supposed to be a light in the middle of the dark winter," Otto replied. "I'm hoping to find it and take some home with me."

Badger scratched his head thoughtfully. "I doubt I can be of much help. I spend the winter sleeping and I don't care much about light. It's easier to steal – I mean, store – apples in the dusk," he said. "But this Christmas sounds nice. Might it be something tasty to eat?" Badger was imagining a soft, slow-baked kind of Christmas with earthworm frosting. The thought made his mouth water.

Otto smiled and shook his head. "I don't think Christmas is something to eat".

Badger gazed at the lengthening shadows in the woods and asked cautiously, "Would you like to have supper with me? I'll be hibernating soon, but I seem to have gathered quite a lot of food. There's more than enough to share."

"With pleasure!" Otto answered in delight. "It's been a long time since my last meal."

To Badger's amazement, Otto built a small fire in the clearing and pulled out a teapot.

Badger admired the flames and served Otto some red apples, considerately keeping any rotten ones for himself. He'd enjoy them later with honey and lingonberries and he'd hide the *really* worm-ridden ones in his burrow, just in case he woke mid-winter in need of a little something.

The pair sat warming their toes by the fire, drinking tea and exchanging stories. Badger told Otto about his marvellous many-chambered burrow and the nosy crow in the pine tree next door.

Otto said Crow sounded like someone at home called Little Grump and Badger listened in fascination to Otto's colourful tales of sea voyages; he had never seen the sea. They were still gazing into the flickering campfire as night fell over the forest.

"You're very welcome to stay the night," Badger suggested. "The guest chamber in the south wing is most comfortable. I padded it myself with moss."

"Thank you. I'd like to stay," said Otto. The autumn night was cooling rapidly and he was tired.

As Badger waddled sleepily into his burrow, Otto watched the glowing embers of their fire. Would Christmas glow as beautifully? Would it be kept in a lantern or would it be too big and heavy to move? If it could light up the whole winter, it must be enormous, he thought.

As the fire faded, the scent of smoke drifted through the dark forest.

3. Kekri, King of the Forest

Autumn painted the forest with its grandest palette of colours. Blazing yellows and reds gleamed against the bright blue sky. Otto paused to marvel at the crimson bilberry leaves and the rowans' majestic hues. A ripe, woody fragrance scented the air.

Otto had left Badger's lovely home a number of days ago and was now heading steadily northward, using the sun as a compass. Each evening the sun set earlier, and he watched the night stars for unusual flashes of light.

One morning he stopped to ask some great tits fluttering past if they had heard of Christmas.

"I know what Christmas is," one of the birds assured him. "It's a big sheaf of oats."

"Is it spectacularly bright? Does it glow?" Otto asked, puzzled.

"Glow?" the bird mused, its head on one side.

"I haven't heard of anything like that," another chirped.

A third cried enthusiastically, "Glowing oats! How exciting!"

The other birds were so carried away with the image of glowing oats that they were soon all shrieking happily together.

"What would happen if you ate glowing oats? Would they shine right through your stomach?" one asked.

"You'd glide about the sky like a giant firefly!" another twittered.

"You could drop glowing oat-balls onto rabbits," a plump bird went on, almost bursting with excitement.

"Or we could hang glowing oat flakes around our nests for decoration! Everyone would be jealous!"

That made the birds laugh so hard one of them nearly fell off its branch.

The great tits chirped tales of different people and creatures. Several of them said they had seen lights, but none of them seemed to remember where, or what they had been like.

A pair of willow tits said they thought Christmas was a big delicious suet ball. A heated debate ensued and Otto decided it was best to continue his journey.

As dawn broke the next day, Otto walked yawning through the frosty forest. The night had been cold, but luckily he had a woollen blanket in his backpack that kept him snuggly warm even in the coldest temperatures. He had brewed blueberry tea over his morning campfire and picked some mushrooms to eat.

The new day softened the frost on the flowers into little dewdrops that vanished in the wind by the afternoon. As he walked, Otto thought up new verses for his travelling song. Shrews scurried along the path beside him and the birds seemed restless.

All of a sudden the forest fell silent. Through the trees Otto could make out something big, dark and steaming. Branches began to sway, and Otto realised that the darkness was alive.

An enormous figure, like an uprooted tree, crashed through the woods towards Otto. Moss and rope-like roots hung from the advancing creature. Its arms looked like thick branches, and the sparse fur on its back stuck out in all directions. It had dull eyes and spruce seedlings growing from its ears. Two dozy mice were sitting on its head.

The creature stopped in front of Otto. A gust of wind seemed to stream from its mouth and the ground resounded as it roared:

Twig-sized man, make way for me,
The forest's mighty King Kekri,
Prince of harvests bountiful,
Bearer of all things plentiful!

Otto stared in fright at Kekri, who loomed before him. He stank like a dog that had spent a week paddling in stagnant water.

"Forgive me," Otto began, his voice quivering only a little. "I didn't know I was in your way. I am travelling to the north to find the light of Christmas."

Kekri swept a fern out of his eyes and peered down with irritation at Otto.

> Listen, puny man in grey,
> Move along, be on your way!
> Christmas doesn't reign round here.
> Find Father Yule and his reindeer.

Otto wondered what this mighty creature might know about Christmas, and apologised once more. "O Lofty One," he began, and saw immediately that Kekri liked this formal address. "I did not intend to trespass in your kingdom. I am on my way north to find the secret light of Christmas. I will continue immediately, but if Your Majesty should wish to help me find my way, I would be ever so grateful." He added a slight bow.

Kekri weighed the words of the stumpy creature at his feet. He did not want to interrupt his march towards the forest's annual celebrations. They were in his honour, after all. He had stopped to be fed and praised at numerous gatherings already, but the forest was large, and all its residents should be given the opportunity to thank their king.

But there was something about the traveller that appealed to Kekri's muddy mind. It was touching that such a meagre little mushroom recognised his mightiness – despite his ridiculous talk of Christmas.

Stepping with dignity past the little grey man, Kekri bellowed:

March north three miles,
Then repeat six times.
Spy the swaying lights
From up in the heights.

Go, seek your Christmas,
Light your life of grey.
May you find plenty
Along the windy way!

His booming voice rang in Otto's ears. If he had understood Kekri's clue correctly, he should keep walking for a distance of six times three miles and look out for swaying lights from a hilltop.

Pleased with himself, Kekri rumbled across the ground and disappeared into the forest, which crumpled and crashed around him, the sleepy mice rocking on his shoulders.

4. A Humming Glow Worm

So far Otto's autumn journey had been sunny and colourful, but now the grey sky sighed as clouds gathered. The light took refuge behind them, and gusts of wind shook the treetops. Birds fell silent. Bugs crawled beneath rocks and tree stumps, waiting for the rain to pass. The only sounds were the cold wind whistling through the forest and the light patter of raindrops. It wasn't long before a crash of thunder turned the rain into a downpour.

The paths became muddy. Raindrops pounded painfully against Otto's eyes and nose. His soft boots were soaked through and the biting wind snuck down the woollens around his neck. He needed to find shelter. Soon, he discovered a small empty cave at the base of a large cliff with dry hay and cones inside. He went in and lifted several spruce boughs to cover the entrance. He quickly started a fire using flints, and hung up his tunic and boots to dry. He felt relieved and snug inside the cave, listening to the raging storm from under his warm woollen blanket.

While small forest dwellers hurried to find holes and hollows to shelter from the storm, large animals could only stand in the rain. A moose on the edge of the forest stood patiently, dreaming about building a moose nest and hoping it would soon be dry again.

When the rain finally stopped, twilight was creeping into the forest. Otto parted the makeshift branch door and sniffed the warming air. A glimmer on the horizon promised that it would not rain tomorrow. The misty forest was peaceful. While Otto debated whether to continue on or wait for dawn, he heard a faint humming from far away.

He packed his backpack and clambered out of the cave, trying to locate the sound, which was growing louder. He set off, tracking it through the woods. As he wound along the path to the top of the cliff, he saw something astonishing in the valley below: a small light was swaying through the mist. He remembered Kekri's verse: *Spy the swaying lights from up in the heights…*

Otto climbed onto a stump to get a better view. Another small light appeared behind the first, and then another, until a whole line of glimmering lanterns was swinging through the valley, carried along by invisible marchers. The procession wound along the path like an enormous glow worm and Otto hurried down after it. The line of light moved briskly, and he heard the humming change into a song with words he didn't recognise. When he reached the end of the lights he could see the marchers better. They were little forest mupples carrying lanterns on sticks.

There are many kinds of mupples. Otto had met beach mupples on his sea voyages and desert mupples when he crossed the Equator. Once he had seen a very rare hermit mupple who lived in his own hole in the mountains, surrounded by three hundred other hermit mupples, each with their own hole.

These forest mupples had round heads with small button ears. Their little eyes were lively, their muzzles narrow and their powerful noses were always sniffing the air. A round, bottle-shaped body spread out beneath non-existent shoulders and their legs were short but nimble. A tail waved happily from each broad bottom. Mupples all around the world sang the same song language, which they had inherited from their ancestors.

Otto followed them, not wanting to interrupt their happy song. The procession continued, winding through the forest and illuminating the lowest branches.

All of a sudden the mupple at the rear sensed something out of the ordinary and turned cautiously to look behind him. Otto waved in greeting, but the mupple was so startled he let out an ear-splitting, "EEEK!"

Soon all of them stood gaping at the unexpected traveller, while the startled one gathered himself, nervously brushing his fur.

"Forgive me. I didn't mean to alarm you," Otto began. "I'm Otto. I come from the coast and I'm travelling north to find the secret light of Christmas."

The creatures tilted their heads and sniffed the air to determine the visitor's real intentions.

Otto continued carefully, "I saw your lovely lanterns from the cliff top. Mighty King Kekri told me that a procession of swaying lights would lead me towards Christmas. Might you be able to help?"

A whisper ran through them and one stepped closer to Otto.

"Greetings, friend from the coast. If King Kekri, our bountiful forest guardian, has guided you to us, you are welcome to join us. We have been gathering delicacies for our Harvest Festival but now we're returning to our village. The trip will take all night, but we have lanterns to light the way."

"Thank you very much!" Otto rejoiced. "I will gladly join you."

The mupples got back into line.

"My name is Sage Sinervo," the mupple said, raising his lantern. "You are most welcome to join our travel song. It hastens the journey."

The procession set off again, beginning a new song. Otto didn't understand a word of it. Nonetheless the line of lights wound through the night forest with Otto at its tail.

5. The Mupples and the Hazytales

As dawn broke, Otto could see the mupples' village on the edge of the forest. Small lanterns surrounded a sheltered clearing where peculiar trees appeared to be growing. Lower down, a stream glided over stones, and a moss-covered rock muffled the roar of the large waterfall.

There were no huts, but little residents bustled everywhere. Tiny mupple children somersaulted on the grass, and fully-grown mupples ran around carrying tools. Some shouted in greeting when they saw the line of lights emerging from the forest, and more popped out of little underground holes to welcome their friends.

Sinervo removed his lantern from the stick and hung it alongside others that encircled the village. Turning to Otto, he bowed with a paw on his chest and said proudly, "Welcome to our village."

Otto bowed in return. Soon a crowd of curious, whispering villagers gathered around him. Sinervo introduced him and then gestured towards a mupple who had appeared wearing a white apron.

"This is my wife, Happy Hellevi. If you will be our guest, she will show you where to sleep. You are more than welcome, although this is a very busy time for us. We are preparing for King Kekri's visit."

Hellevi handed Otto a freshly baked mushroom pasty with such a warm smile that Otto blushed.

"Welcome," she said. "Sinervo will show you round the village while I prepare the guest room for you."

"Thank you," Otto replied, looking around.

Whispering among themselves, the mupples cast curious glances at Otto as they returned to work. They darted about the forest, climbing onto stumps and stones, craning their necks, pricking their ears and sniffing the air.

Sinervo, who appeared to be their leader, led Otto through the village towards the huge root of a pointed tree, where a mupple with tufts of green fur sat daydreaming.

"This is my brother Poet Pauli. He may be able to help you. He's had more conversations with the hazytales than any of us."

Otto had no time to reply before Sinervo carried on, "Please excuse me. I have to check on the builders." And with that he was off, trotting over to a group who were digging enormous roots out of the ground.

Otto didn't know what hazytales were, but Pauli looked pleasant and peaceful, so he decided to introduce himself.

Poet Pauli was an unusual mupple. He loved dreaming and writing poetry. He worked alongside the other mupples in the daytime, but in the evening when the others were busy playing games together, Pauli would sink into his own thoughts and compose poems about the moon. The other mupples thought he was a bit crazy.

Otto pulled the battered old postcard out of his pocket and explained that he was searching for the light of Christmas. Pauli nodded, and after a moment he said, "I've heard of Christmas too."

"What is it?" Otto asked excitedly. "Is it a huge lantern?"

"I'm not quite sure," Pauli replied. "The hazytales have talked about it, but their tales don't progress very quickly."

"But you've heard of Christmas?" Otto asked hopefully.

"Yes," Pauli said. "I think Christmas sounds peaceful. Like something you could hug while you're watching the stars…"

Pauli's voice grew softer and softer until he seemed to be murmuring to himself.

Before Pauli slipped back into a daydream, Otto asked hurriedly, "Where can I find these hazytales who tell stories of Christmas?"

Pauli didn't have a chance to answer before the pointed tree they were sitting on shifted slowly. From high in its crown came a musing voice:

"Ah, Christmas," the tree sighed.

Otto jumped and stepped backwards. It wasn't a tree at all, but rather some sort of tall grey creature. Eyes peered from its narrow head and it seemed to smile at Otto.

"I remember Christmas," the creature said slowly. "We used to have… er…"

It looked at Otto, who couldn't tell if it was going to continue.

Pauli said calmly, "This is a hazytale. They are extremely slow. It may take them half a day to utter two sentences. I hope you're not in a hurry, because if you want to gather wisdom from a hazytale, you'll have to sit here with me for some time."

The grey creature roused itself a little and continued in a soft voice, "I'll tell you about Christmas. I'll telllllllll… Hmmm… First some coffee."

The hazytale lifted an arm draped with beard-moss and lichens. Slowly he raised a pot that hung from something branch-like at his side. In his other hand he held a wooden cup, which seemed to have grown attached to him. Very slowly the

hazytale poured steaming coffee into the cup and stirred it steadily with a pine branch.

Otto sat beside Pauli, watching the strange creature, which was about the same height as a medium-sized spruce. Twigs sprouted from its greyed skin and beard-moss from its neck. Enormous roots spread from its trunk towards the ground, and its legs were hidden in a root-tangle skirt. It didn't look very mobile.

Pauli leaned back, lacing his fingers on his stomach. "The hazytales and the forest mupples have lived together for many years. Their ancestors set off long, long ago on a trip around the world – from just over there to the west where they were born. Through all the generations they have only advanced a few miles!"

"They don't seem the travelling sort," Otto said with a smile.

"I'll say!" Pauli laughed. "Long ago, hazytales were a lively, talkative folk. They told each other so many stories that they ran out. When the tales dried up the hazytales started to slow down, so they set off on a trip to gather new stories."

"Have they always looked like that?" Otto asked, glancing at the lingonberry sprays sprouting from the hazytale's shoulders.

"Not at all," Pauli replied. "When they slowed down, forest plants began to take root around them. Without our help, they quickly get stuck in one place."

Otto looked over at the mupples busily digging. He realised that they were detaching the hazytales' long roots, which criss-crossed the ground.

"The roots form hollows in the ground where forest mupples have lived for decades," Pauli explained. "Sometimes we let them grow for structural support and the hazytales rest for a few years in the same place. One year they were feeling particularly sprightly and we moved the village about ten metres from the forest edge."

While the mupples bustled around them, the hazytales didn't seem interested in anything but their own coffee pots. They savoured life's peaceful moments. They didn't want to rush in case they missed a story. After all, they were on an exciting trip around the world!

Otto looked at the hazytale beside him, who had dozed off while sipping coffee.

"That happens a lot," Pauli said. "They communicate with each other through their root systems while they sleep, so little naps are commonplace."

"Will he wake up and continue our conversation?" Otto asked.

"Probably," said Pauli. He reached over for the hazytale's coffee cup and poured a couple of splashes into two smaller beakers. "Let's have a little drink while we wait," he said. "Otherwise we might drift off, too!"

Sipping coffee, they watched the hazytale dozing, a blissful expression on its face.

43

6. An Evening Underground

Pauli tried to recall everything the hazytales had told him about Christmas.

"Christmas is celebrated in the darkest time of the year, but preparations start in the autumn so its light brightens all of winter."

Pauli had paused to think if there was anything to add when the hazytale beside him finally woke and began to speak: "The old man, Father Yule… hmmm…" it began.

Otto started. He remembered that Kekri had said something about Father Yule: *Find Father Yule and his reindeer.*

The hazytale looked at Otto with bright eyes and went on, "Father Yule, on the fells – there's the heart of Christmas. At the darkest… hmmm… you'll hear his call. There'll be light… Let's have coffee."

The hazytale bent over its cup again, the pots clinking at its side. Sleepily it sank back into its own world, stirring its drink and humming to itself.

Pauli had started on his own project: working straw into a beautiful decoration. "I don't think you'll get much more out of that hazytale," he said, "but you're welcome to stay and wait."

"Could I help somehow? That looks fun," Otto asked, studying Pauli as he threaded pieces of straw onto a string.

"Of course," Pauli said, raising the decoration so that it swung lightly in the breeze. "This is called a himmeli. I'm making it for the Harvest Festival we hold to honour Mighty Kekri and ensure a good harvest next year."

"I see," Otto nodded. "It looks tricky."

Pauli taught Otto the way to make himmelis. While he did, he told him more about the forest mupples and their village. When day darkened into night, Happy Hellevi invited Otto into their underground dwelling. Otto followed her down some steps that were carved from hazytale roots.

He was amazed at the huge common areas and small sleeping cubbies. The mupples shared a spacious kitchen and in it tall wooden shelves overflowed with marvellous jugs and jars, cups and canisters, bowls and basins. Dried roots and herbs hung side by side in neat bundles from the ceiling. The pantry door was painted a joyful red. Hammocks hung from the kitchen ceiling where mothers rocked their babies to sleep. Some mupples were making lingonberry preserve at a long table, and in front of the stove a grandma was weaving beard-lichen into yarn.

Otto climbed a ladder and proudly hung up the small himmeli he had crafted, alongside other handsome ornaments that swung in the breeze.

Otto found that mupples consider it a matter of honour to serve guests a delicious meal. Platters of succulent pies and casseroles, beetle eggs and fresh waterfall fish were brought to the table for everyone to share.

"We only have everyday food to offer," Happy Hellevi apologised as she carried a huge bowl to the table. "I hope it's okay."

"Happy's too humble!" one of the mupples shouted.

Sinervo and the others joined in, chanting, "She's the best cook in this forest!"

Happy blushed and served Otto some delicious spruce nuts, which he ate with gusto.

After dinner, some of the mupples played a jumping game, while others continued to bustle around and prepare for

King Kekri's arrival. They were full of energy, but Otto was so tired he couldn't keep his eyes open. He thanked them for their hospitality, bade them good night, and retired to his sleeping cubby, where he fell asleep instantly.

7. The Leaf Fairies' Last Dance

Otto stayed with the forest mupples for several days, but his conversation with the hazytales led no further. They had begun to slip into their winter sleep and uttered only a few words a day.

The wind began to bite as Otto followed the stream away from the mupples' village, heading north towards the fells of Lapland. He stopped at a small cove for lunch, which he shared with some curious trout. He knew his fisherman's luck came from his respect for water life, but today he left the trout to play in peace. He plunged further into the dim frosty woods. The only sounds that reached him were a distant crow's caw and the creak of swaying trees.

Otto sang to bolster his spirits.

> *The welcoming mupples*
> *Remain behind.*
> *Now a silent world*
> *Cloaked in moss and vine…*
> *Where leads this path*
> *and this trip of mine?*

The path opened abruptly into a clearing where the wind whipped fiercely. Otto was amazed to notice a green glow at the base of a large spruce tree. At first it was just a glimmer, but the more he stared, the brighter it grew. What could shine so fiercely? He stretched out a tentative hand to investigate and a small clear voice warned, "I wouldn't do that if I were you!"

Otto spun around.

There was no one there! Had he really heard something?

He stretched his hand towards the green light again.

"If you want to keep your fingers, pull them back quick!"

"Who's there?" Otto cried, turning around again.

A small aspen leaf swaying back and forth at eye-level exclaimed, "I didn't mean to snap at you, but you were about to touch the goblin's gold! He's terribly attached to his treasure and he's very excitable. When he gets mad he can swallow tree stumps or little travellers whole!"

Otto gaped at the talking leaf, and couldn't utter a word. It swayed in the breeze and went on in a musical voice, "You're not from around here, are you? Come a bit closer."

Otto stepped closer. Now he saw a tiny figure dangling from the branch, her dress spread around her like an aspen leaf.

"I'm Niiu, a leaf fairy. I suppose you haven't met anyone like me before?"

He looked at her in astonishment. He could see her tiny face at the top of the stem. Her golden hair was twined around a branch and she swung her skirts with graceful, thread-like arms.

"My name's Otto," he finally managed to say. "You're the first leaf fairy I've ever met."

"How thrilling!" Niiu cried. "It's always fun to meet travellers. And today's a splendid day to meet us because we're just about to start our farewell dance. You came at the perfect time to watch."

"Farewell dance?" Otto asked cautiously.

"The leaf fairies' last dance of autumn," Niiu replied. "Once we've danced down to the ground, we leave this life."

Otto gazed sadly at the little fairy and asked, "You only live for one summer?"

"I live a whole life, birth and death," Niiu said, smiling, a tremor in her voice. "In spring the sun warms us into life, all summer we sing and dance in the trees, and in autumn they fall asleep and we perform our farewell dance. Next spring, new leaf fairies will be born. That's nature's cycle; there's no reason to be sad about it."

Otto looked at the little figure quivering in the wind, her dress shimmering gold in the sun. He sat down on the edge of the meadow to keep her company. She glowed with such great joy as she described her short life that Otto felt his heart about to burst with admiration.

The trees began to hum along with the wind, and Niiu's eyes lit up.

"We're starting soon," she said. "I'm glad you're here to watch. Remember to avoid the goblin. He checks his treasure every day, so wait till evening's darkness to continue your journey."

"Thank you for the warning. I'll do that," Otto said. "And thank you for allowing me to watch your last dance."

Niiu's eyes sparkled as she swished her skirts in reply.

The humming from the trees intensified and Otto leaned back to watch as the leaf fairies began their performance.

The sun was already at the horizon. The forest glowed gold, the fairies sparkling like gems on the branches as the trees hummed a soothing melody. Dewdrops tinkled as they slipped from tall grass to the ground and the grass resonated like violins, until soon the whole forest had joined in the symphony.

Then the leaf fairies began their dance. One after another they dropped gently from the branches, spreading their shimmering skirts in the breeze. The air filled with fairies, and Otto watched, mesmerised. They radiated a joy of life and a beauty he had never experienced before.

Now it was Niiu's turn. She closed her eyes and let go of the branch. The wind carried her high up into the treetops, before she twirled down towards earth.

On reaching the ground the fairies melted into one another and the trees sighed as they gathered strength to face the winter cold. The sun set, and silence settled over the forest while the moon rose in the sky.

Wistfully, Otto continued on his way.

8. Frosted Bear

The night was bright and the wind had subsided. Otto looked at the clear, black sky with its twinkling stars. The world felt vast beneath it.

Frost spread over the forest. Dewdrops froze into strings of pearls, moss became a sparkling blanket and the cold air chilled pine trunks into great silver pillars. The whole wood glistened in the moonlight and was so quiet that even thinking a small thought felt like speaking aloud.

Otto tried to find the North Star. First he looked for the constellation of Ursa Major, the Great Bear, to guide him north.

Suddenly something big and black blocked the constellation from view: the starlight lit up a fur coat sprinkled with glittering frost and Otto could see a huge *real* bear standing before him.

The bear looked at Otto. In her eyes he was just a small grey dot, but the enormous creature responded to the stranger with quiet curiosity. Otto did not look threatening to the bear who, it turned out, was respected by the whole forest, even the mighty King Kekri.

Otto was afraid she might pop him into her mouth. Should he have stayed at home after all and been flattened to the size of a mouse dropping under a collapsed roof?

The bear was big, even for a bear. She was used to seeing forest dwellers trembling in her presence, but Otto was different. The bear was intrigued by the flash in Otto's eyes and above all, by his absurd hat.

"Tomorrow it will snow," she said in a soft voice. "I recommend you look for shelter or you will be buried. Your path will vanish."

The great bear's thoughtfulness took Otto by surprise. He replied, "Thank you for the advice, good friend. My name is Otto. I was intending to sleep in a hollow spruce."

"That doesn't sound good," the bear mused. "Where are you headed?"

"I'm heading north," Otto told her. "I'm looking for Father Yule who I hope can tell me about the secret light of Christmas."

She looked at Otto with interest. "One time, long ago, I met Father Yule," the bear reminisced. "He advised me how to become a good leader for the forest. I'm sure he will be able to tell you about Christmas and the winter lights." The bear dropped her forepaws to the ground and looked at little Otto. "Why don't you tell me more about your adventures," she said gently. "I can offer you a warm place for the night so you don't get buried under the snow."

"That's very kind of you," Otto said with relief. How very lucky, he thought, that the bear had not even considered having him for a snack.

The bear lifted Otto onto her back and set off walking calmly through the forest. Otto told her about his journey and the bear laughed when he described the bustling mupples. The new friends also discovered they shared a love of fishing. "Nothing can beat the feeling when your wait is rewarded and you hook a big fat trout!" said the bear. The friends chatted merrily as snowflakes drifted down from the black sky.

By the time its den came into view at the base of a cliff, the path was already hard to see under the snow. The bear lowered

Otto to the ground at the entrance and shook snowflakes from her fur. Otto's hat had fallen over his eyes from the weight of the snow and he shook the powder off. The bear stretched and showed Otto which direction to take when he woke in the morning.

"I sleep deeply," the bear explained. "I may not wake for a few months. You are welcome to stay as long as you wish, but if you continue your trip now, while there's still some daylight, I believe you'll find what you're seeking." She gazed at the snowy pines and said, "If you're lucky, you may bump into the lonttis."

"Lonttis?" Otto echoed.

"The lontti folk know Father Yule and, if they're feeling talkative, they will advise you on the route north.

"Will I meet them along the way?" Otto asked, looking doubtfully at the dark forest.

"Very likely," the bear replied. "They may be hard to find, but keeping an open mind helps. There are lonttis everywhere, but they're champions at hiding." The bear continued, "I'm quite sure you'll encounter them. They hate to miss exciting travellers."

The bear clambered into her warm den with Otto following behind her, and the friends exchanged fishing tales side-by-side until both fell asleep. Only the bear's muffled snoring broke the snowy silence of the forest.

When Otto crawled outside in the morning, the brightness of the snow was blinding. It had turned the forest into a land of lumpy white shapes, and he had to think for a minute to remember which way the path went. Then he pulled his hat over his ears and left the bear's den behind. Although the fresh snow was light, it was still hard for little Otto to trudge through. He sang to speed himself along, his breath steaming in the cold air.

A veil of white,
A cloak of snow,
With Otto nearly
Trapped below.

Snow sheets and mounds
Loom low and high,
Now gone the line
'Tween land and sky.

9. The Secret of the Snow Lonttis

After walking for half a day, Otto decided to take a break. He stamped out a small resting place in the snow and sat down to light a fire. He ate some preserved mushrooms with a cup of tea. All the wild berries were now buried beneath the snow and he couldn't see anywhere to fish. He wondered how long his food would last.

Winters on the coast weren't very snowy. Otto had never seen so much of it before. He dug up a handful and blew cold crystals from his hand, admiring how they sparkled in the sun.

Just then something moved. Otto was sure he'd seen motion in the corner of his eye, but there was nothing nearby. Still, something seemed different about the drift beside him.

When he poked it with a finger, the snow felt warm.

"Ow!" it said.

Otto snatched his finger away.

The pile gave a frustrated snort. "Bother! You wouldn't have noticed me if I hadn't twitched!"

Otto looked at it in astonishment as it shifted and went on, "Pretty good snowfall today, wouldn't you say? Had to hurry to pull on my snow coat!"

"Don't talk to him!" an irritable voice hissed from a pine branch above.

"Oh, surely it doesn't matter now. He's already noticed me," the first voice retorted.

Peering closely, Otto made out a round face and dark button eyes in the snowdrift.

"Who are you?" it asked in a friendly voice. "I smell blueberry tea… might there be a sip for me?"

The nervous snow heap on the branch overhead hissed, "Don't take anything from that strange creature! You don't know where he's been! Be quiet and maybe he'll go away!"

"Pay no attention to him," the first voice said. "He's always a grump. I think you look perfectly fine."

Otto introduced himself cautiously and watched as the pile began to take on the shape of some sort of creature.

"Forgive my curiosity, but… are you a lontti?" Otto asked.

"No need to apologise," the creature replied. "Yes, we are lonttis – snow lonttis today, to be precise. We change name according to where we happen to be. Yesterday we were moss lonttis."

"I'm actually a stick lontti," the other one sniffed.

The peculiar creature blended in completely with the snow. Its body shaped itself to the ground and the branches, and you could only just distinguish two dark eyes and a broad smile.

The irritable lontti was obviously nervous, but Otto was beginning to make out its figure on the pine branch above.

When Otto asked if they could help him find Father Yule, the first lontti drew itself upwards and cried, "What a coincidence! We know the bearded old chap well!" Then it bent closer to Otto and wheedled, "How about that blueberry tea?"

Otto served him a cup and the lontti continued, "Father Yule is our old friend. In fact, we lonttis are almost like his secret spies."

The irritable lontti above hissed, "Don't tell him! If he finds out, the secret won't be a secret any more!"

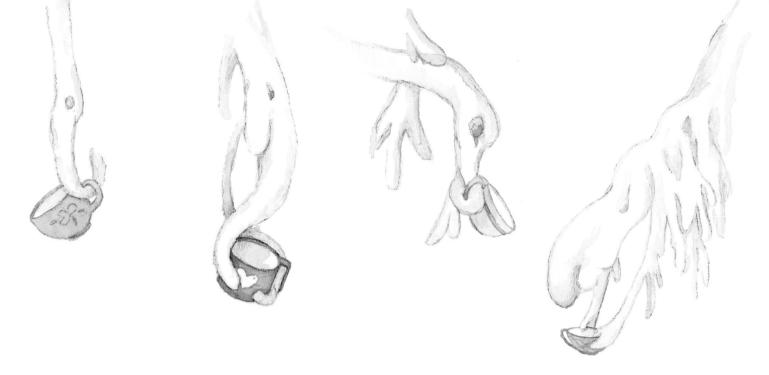

But the tea-sipping lontti just looked at Otto calmly and continued talking. "We pass on information to the old fellow about what the forest dwellers are up to." He stretched his arms importantly. "There isn't a single forest without lonttis lounging on its branches! Not a single lake without lonttis sprawled on its beach. No meadow without grass lonttis, no cottage without firewood lonttis. No—"

Otto interrupted, "You're certainly indispensable. I would be ever so grateful if you could tell me where I can find old Father Yule."

"He sits up on the fells," the lontti said. "Take the shortcut along the lake to the open plains and head north from there."

The lontti's clear directions surprised Otto; the purpose of his long journey suddenly seemed within reach.

The irritable lontti on the branch above had calmed down a bit, and asked, "Might there be a cup of tea left?" It extended its own cup towards Otto.

Otto poured it some tea, and soon many little cups were being held out towards him as all the lonttis came out of hiding.

"Is it blueberry tea?" a voice called from the base of a pine.

"Why is he wearing such a goofy cap?" another wondered.

"Is there enough tea for me too?" yet another called.

Otto politely shared his tea, and in appreciation the lonttis continued chatting about Father Yule.

When Otto mused aloud how difficult it would be to wade through the high snowdrifts, a lontti on a rock suddenly shouted, "I've got it!" It whispered something to the lontti beside it, who passed on the message to the one next to him.

So on it went, until a question rang out from far away: "*Nose* shoes?"

"SNOWshoes!" the first lontti shouted back.

Perplexed, Otto looked at the lontti who, bursting with excitement, said, "Wait till you see! We have a splendid

invention that was originally developed to help the early lonttis move about."

Soon two sieve-like ovals with straps were passed to Otto.

"These are snowshoes," said the lontti on the rock. "Try them! They let you walk easily on snow."

Otto strapped them on and took a hesitant step. "I think they work!"

"Of course they work," said the lontti beside him.

"These will make my journey much easier." He thanked them, and the lonttis chuckled with pleasure, feeling important and helpful.

After sharing one more pot of blueberry tea, Otto waved goodbye and continued on his way, singing happily:

Who'd ever guess,
Sitting in the snow,
That right beside you
Wriggle lontti toes!

Every lump and bump,
Each stone and stump,
Branch short or wide,
Many secrets hide.

10. Booming Burl

Otto headed out of the forest towards the lake the lonttis had indicated. By the time he reached it, the sun had already set. The farther north he went, the shorter the days became.

He moved lightly over the snow with his new snowshoes. The moon and stars lit the land more brightly here than they did in the forest depths. The edge of the water was lightly frozen, with patches of thicker ice. Otto tested it. The ice tilted and the water below surged like a wind-blown meadow.

Otto saw something gleaming in the centre of the lake. He circled a small cove to get a better view. In the middle of the lake blazed a bright fire, as round as a ball. Otto stared at it in amazement. Soon it began to move slowly back and forth. It couldn't be an ice fisherman's fire – the ice wasn't strong enough to hold anyone. The glowing orb floated eerily above the ice as the lake creaked and groaned.

A hearty voice snapped Otto out of his thoughts: "No need to let that spook you. It'll stay there on the lake."

"Excuse me?" Otto stammered, turning quickly.

Beside Otto crouched a troll-sized creature, gathering tinkling ice lanterns from the base of thick reeds on the shore. "Those will-o'-the-wisps are just mischief makers, trying to lure passers-by onto the thin ice. We know better!" The troll straightened up and said, "Haven't seen you around here before."

"I'm on my way to the northern plains," Otto replied. "My name is Otto. The lonttis directed me this way."

"Those lazy things! I bet they forgot to mention how hard the trip north would be for such a tiny fellow."

The man was much bigger than Otto. He had a large nose, sturdy hands and muscular legs. He wore a fur cap on his head and several knives dangled at his waist. He had red diamonds on his sweater, which stretched over his round stomach.

"Will-o'-the-wisps are the least of your worries. They tease and tempt, but they're harmless if you ignore them." The figure extended his great mitt, which Otto squeezed. "Name's Booming Burl. Just call me Boomer. Help me gather these lanterns and I'll give you a ride to the plains. It's quite a way and I don't think you'll get there very fast on foot."

Otto was pleased with this deal. While Boomer showed him how to lift the lanterns, he explained that he came here to gather them every winter for the midwinter celebrations held in his village.

Boomer was loud, but very friendly. When they had collected great armloads of lanterns, he led Otto towards a sleigh attached to a gigantic horse, which snorted when it saw Boomer. The horse had a thick blond mane and sturdy legs. It pawed the snow, eager to be on its way.

"Pookie will take us back to the village," Boomer said proudly, giving the horse a hearty thump. "You won't find a faster or stronger mare anywhere. We'll be home before dark tomorrow. Hop in and we'll be off!"

He sat down in the great sleigh and grabbed the reins. Otto removed his snowshoes and climbed up beside him under warm fur rugs. Boomer clicked his tongue and the horse set off.

Snow sprayed as the sleigh sped swiftly through the cold night.

Boomer smiled in the moonlight and told Otto about his village. The Klupu were strong, merry people who had lived on the plains of Lapland for centuries.

Otto told Boomer about his seafaring adventures and his long trip north. With the stars twinkling above, Otto found it hard to keep his eyes open and before long he fell fast asleep.

It was twilight when the sleigh arrived at the Klupu village; there was just a faint pink streak on the horizon. Otto started awake to see a cluster of great red houses. Boomer stopped Pookie outside one of them and Otto stepped down, gazing all around.

Boomer set the lanterns beside an enormous cartwheel that leaned against a house.

"You slept for quite a while," said Boomer. "Come in! Let's see if we can rustle up some grub!"

Otto followed Boomer into a large room. In its centre was a long wooden table lit by a glowing oil lamp. Rag rugs covered the floor and in the corner a cosy fire glowed. A round, red-cheeked woman stepped forward carrying a basket that smelled of freshly baked bread.

"Well, well! Look what the wind blew in!" she said, and looked at Otto. "What little chap did you pick up on the way?"

Otto removed his hat and introduced himself with a bow.

"This is Hulda, roundest lady in town," Boomer said heartily.

Hulda chuckled and winked at Otto. "You may be small, but you have more manners than all the men in this village put together! Have a seat!"

Boomer removed his hat and sat at the head of the table. Otto found a seat on a bench. Soon other villagers arrived and the table was filled with large, loud Klupus who'd been working all day in the woods, as well as Klupu women and children, who were as loud as the biggest men.

Hulda carried more baskets of bread to the table, some of the loaves nearly the same size as Otto. Juicy meat, berry preserves, fresh fish and big pitchers of ale also appeared, and the Klupus tucked in. The room buzzed with chatter, singing and laughter that made the rafters ring.

"Welcome to our village," Boomer said to Otto. "We're glad you could join us."

The festivities went on for a long time. The villagers decorated the room and the children played games. After dinner, instruments were found and soon the whole house rang with music. Some Klupus danced so hard the floor shook.

Boomer was soon dozing in his chair, which was taken as a good omen. "We believe that the faster the host falls asleep, the better the harvest the following year," one villager explained. "And if the host snores, there'll be a great harvest next year!"

Just at that moment, Boomer started to snore gently. Everyone cheered – which woke him up. He rubbed his eyes, and looked at Otto. "Do you want to come to the sauna? You'll get your feet clean and your head clear, after a long day!"

"I'd love to," Otto replied.

11. Little Hiss

A group of Klupus strolled with Otto towards a grey wooden hut. They squeezed into a tiny dressing room and took off all their clothes before entering the sauna, a deliciously hot room filled with steam. In the dim light, Otto could see the glow of a great stove with a fire crackling in its furnace. A wood-scent filled the air.

Boomer picked up a big ladle and tossed water onto the stove until the heat stung their cheeks and noses. Each ladleful created a burst of swirling steam.

Every now and then some Klupus would dart outside to roll in the snow, then hurry back inside for more steam.

After the others left, Otto and Boomer stayed a while longer, sitting on the bench together.

Boomer waved the ladle at the stove and said, "The last throws are for Little Hiss-of-the-Sauna."

Otto looked at the stove in wonder.

Boomer explained, "Little Hiss is the spirit of the sauna. The last ladlefuls are always for him. That keeps him satisfied and we get good hot saunas all the following year."

"Does Little Hiss live in the stove?" Otto asked.

"Under it, although if it gets too hot he sometimes climbs onto the stove wall."

Otto peered through the steamy gloom to see if he could spot a living creature under the stove. He couldn't see anything in the blackness.

"He's a shy, tricky little chap," Boomer continued, "but I know a way to make him show his face."

Boomer drizzled a long, sizzling ribbon of water onto the stove. The stones glowed and the furnace flared.

When the hiss of the steam subsided, a small voice could be heard from underneath: "Booming Burl, you are the worst kind of trickster yourself!"

A tiny spiky-haired head framed by little protruding ears peeped out from under the stove. Little Hiss was covered all over in dark fur, except for his knees and toes. He leapt nimbly onto the wall to sit down. Otto thought of Little Grump and wondered if he and Little Hiss might be related.

"Terrific sauna you made us," Boomer said to the creature. "One worth boasting about."

Little Hiss studied Otto, his head tilted and his eyes glowing, and said nothing.

Otto thanked him politely for the excellent hot sauna, which made the timid little spirit hiss with pleasure. "Shushhh, it was nothing special…"

"Indeed it was! This sauna is the best anywhere and the credit's all yours!" Boomer raved. "Unbeatable!"

Little Hiss was visibly pleased and remained sitting on the wall, flicking drops of water at the stove. Otto and Boomer stayed in the sauna with the little spirit, and they each shared stories of their adventures, both hot and cold.

When Otto's skin glowed lobster-red, it was time to leave. Boomer filled the sauna bucket with water for the next bathers and thanked Little Hiss again, who jumped down and tucked himself away under the stove.

He waved at Otto and called in his whistling voice, "I wish you luck for your journey. You're welcome to come to my sauna again!"

Otto and Boomer headed back to the house, bright red and clean as whistles.

Boomer thought Otto would need a good pair of skis to reach the northern fells so he took him to meet the most skilful carpenter in the village.

The carpenter was puffing on a pipe in front of his shop. He was even bigger than Boomer, and an imposing beard covered his ruddy face.

"Evening, Boomer! What brings you here?" he growled.

"Evening, carpenter!" Boomer replied warmly. "Apologies for coming round so late, but this little friend of mine is in need of some skis."

Otto extended his hand, which the carpenter pressed gently with his own great hand as he blew smoke into the air. Stroking his whiskers and sizing up Otto, he said, "I don't have any skis in your size, little chap. But if you wait a few days, I'll make some that are just right."

"Thank you so much," Otto said. "How can I repay you?"

"Rumour has it you're quite the storyteller," the carpenter replied. "Why don't you sit with me and speed my work with your tales. I'd like to hear about your adventures on the world seas."

Otto agreed, and then he and Boomer headed home and slept very, very soundly.

Otto spent several days in the lively Klupu village. While he told stories in the carpenter's shop, he whittled little birds from wood shavings and the carpenter said they would make a splendid addition to their festive decorations.

When his skis were finished and Otto had tested them, the villagers helped him prepare for his onward trip. But Boomer seemed uneasy.

"Is something wrong?" Otto asked.

Finally, Boomer told him what he'd been worrying about: a mean creature called Ironworm, the torment of the plains.

"It's a miserable, cruel creature that whispers horrid things," said Boomer. "If you let it, Ironworm will paralyse your mind."

Hulda, who was filling Otto's backpack with food, added, "Don't believe anything Ironworm whispers. You won't see it – it wriggles underground – but if you let dark thoughts enter your mind, it will gain strength."

Otto shivered at the thought of meeting something frightening that he couldn't see, let alone understand. The Klupus assured him that Ironworm would fall silent once Otto reached the fells, and that he would be strong enough to resist its nasty whisperings.

Otto hadn't travelled this far to give up now. He had such a burning desire to find Father Yule and learn about the secret light of Christmas that he set off, full of resolve, skiing north.

12. Ironworm

The carpenter had waxed Otto's skis for speed and he felt as if he were flying over the snowy plains. The polar night had settled over Lapland; the sun was only a fleeting glimmer on the horizon. It was easy to find his way by the light of the stars, but when the clouds gathered into a thick velvet cloak, he had to slow his pace.

The plains reminded him of the ocean, with drifts rolling like waves in the darkness, and he felt a twinge of homesickness so as he travelled, he sang to pass the time:

> *Rolling meadows,*
> *Skis take flight,*
> *Journey on*
> *Through the pitch-black night.*
>
> *So much behind,*
> *What lies ahead?*
> *It sure would be easier*
> *To travel by sled!*
>
> *O north, here I am!*
> *Mesmerise! Dazzle me!*
> *Show me the light*
> *That I so long to see!*

But the darkness continued; days were nights and nights were days. Only a brief light on the horizon revealed when night had passed.

Otto rested every so often, watching the stars twinkle. He wondered whether his home was still in one piece and how Seagull Schooner was doing; whether Little Grump had eaten the cupboard bare and if the fishtails would last till spring.

Home was far away. What if he didn't find the light of Christmas or Father Yule? He would still face an extremely long trip back.

Just then, Otto heard an ominous rumbling under the ground.

He ignored it and kept going. But no matter how quickly his skis flew, the sound intensified. The earth trembled and he saw the snow heaving in the dark.

His voice cracking, Otto shouted into the blackness, "Go away! Get away from here!"

But Ironworm had found Otto. It wriggled under the snow, making the ground shudder. Otto couldn't see it, but he could definitely feel it.

A grim hiss echoed through the dark as Ironworm whispered, "Ssshhhhhhhhhhh. Lisssen to me, sssmall mite. Releasssse those sssski polessss. Rest, ressst, in my sssnow…"

Otto did not answer. Although the worm whispered softly, its words penetrated his ears like a thunderclap.

Valiantly he continued his journey as Ironworm raised clouds of snow around him. Its wriggling made the snow tremble and it felt to Otto as if the worm were larger than an ocean liner.

"Ssshhhh," Ironworm hissed. "Meagre mite in the night. Ssstop ssssenselesss ssskiing. I will fill you with darkness, your heart with gloom. Ssssurrender! Ressst in my ssssnow!"

The worm was hissing right beside Otto, who could see its huge eyes gleaming in the darkness. The relentless stare of those two beacons was more piercing than any light.

Otto turned his eyes away. He focused on home: the soothing beach stones, waves on a summer day and the cheerful calling of seabirds.

But the worm didn't give up.

"Sssshhhhh. Where are you fleeing to, little mite? Skisss can't ssssave you. Darknesss isss at your door. Ressst in my ssssnow forever."

Otto had experienced many things in his life, including gigantic monsters, but Ironworm was different. It had no desire other than to be evil and cruel. He knew it would only go away if he could keep his own thoughts cheery. But it was difficult to think happy thoughts all alone in the darkness.

The land was starting to become hilly, dotted here and there with scrawny pines and bushes. Even though the worm was still whispering, Otto had to rest.

At the base of a small pine he lit his storm lantern. Staring into its bright flame, Otto could feel the worm winding in a circle around him. He thought about his life and his friends. He tried desperately to stay awake, but the demanding journey had taken its toll, and soon he closed his eyes and drifted into a restless sleep. Ironworm grew stronger...

Otto was sitting in the sun at home on his dock when threatening storm clouds gathered on the horizon. He wriggled his toes in the water and watched the pike play among the reeds. Seagull Schooner was gliding towards him from the sea, calling something. But the waves lashed the beach harder. The wind tugged at Schooner's wings, making it difficult to fly. Little Grump sat motionless in the window of Otto's small grey hut. The pike had vanished from the reeds and Schooner shouted again, but Otto didn't hear. The world seemed to be disappearing behind a grey curtain. The sky darkened quickly. Even as the storm swirled about, sound faded, and he felt as if he were falling down something deep. Schooner flapped up to him screaming, "Otto! Wake up!"

Otto started awake. His lantern had gone out and, apart from a dim reddish glow on the horizon, it was pitch black. Ironworm was staring at him with gleaming eyes, hissing hideously. Otto didn't know which way to go.

Then from far off he heard a faint howling. He sat up to listen. Ironworm whistled and rumbled but Otto focused all his energy on trying to make out the new sound: it was a wolf howling. He seized his skis with new determination and set off towards it.

A pack of wolves materialised out of the dark. A big beast with pale fur stopped in front of him, the dim light from the moon reflecting in its grey eyes. In a gentle voice, the wolf said, "There's not much farther to go. Follow my pack and you will be safe."

Otto nodded trustingly in reply. The wolves moved around him and the darkness no longer felt endless. He gathered his strength and skied.

Ironworm followed, spraying clouds of snow. "Sssshhhhh," it hissed irritably. "Where do you think you're going? Shut your eyesssss again! Ressst in my dark snow!"

Otto swung his pole towards the sound and snapped, "Don't you threaten me! No matter what you whisper, I'll keep going!"

The worm seethed with rage but Otto skied on. The wolfpack bayed beside him, paying no attention to Ironworm's nasty hissing. He could see its eyes growing dimmer and its wriggling weaker as he and the wolves sped on through the night.

When the edge of the fells at last loomed before them, the worm became quiet and vanished back underground. Its hissing could no longer be heard.

Otto looked around with relief. The wolves were already far away. Their calls echoed through the night as they disappeared into darkness.

13. A Chatty Reindeer

A line of treeless mountains rose in the light of the slim crescent moon. Finally, the northern fells Otto had been looking for.

Gazing, exhausted, into the dark, at first he didn't notice movement at the foot of the mountain. Only as he glided slowly towards a clearing did he make out hundreds of creatures with antlers.

Gusty had been watching Otto; in the long, monotonous winter he enjoyed looking to see what might emerge from the darkness. But in all his years, he'd never seen a tiny grey fellow like this one. He made a refreshing change from ptarmigans and arctic foxes. It never occurred to the reindeer to be afraid of the little traveller.

"Good evening," Otto said, bowing politely as the herd crowded around him.

So these must be reindeer!

The reindeer standing in front of Otto had legs as narrow as birch branches and a stomach like a great drum. He thought its head looked normal sized, not small, as Little Grump had suggested. The reindeer watched him calmly and kept chewing lichens. Otto wondered if Little Grump might have been right about them being stupid.

"I've travelled a long way to meet Father Yule," Otto said tentatively. "I've heard the light of Christmas can be found on the northern fells. Can you tell me where to go from here?"

The reindeer looked placidly at the little man, who was out of breath but chattering eagerly. Gusty didn't want to tire himself out with too much enthusiasm, but he considered himself a polite reindeer, so he answered promptly. "Good evening, Traveller Otto. I am Gusty and this is my herd – only a few hundred of us. These fells have been our home for many years, but we've also enjoyed the northern lakes, especially in summer. Pleasant place – plentiful shoots and birch sprouts for a light meal. Sometimes too many lemmings. Not that they're a problem, but they get terribly angry if we accidentally munch on one of their legs…"

Otto tried in vain to get a word in edgewise.

"Yes, so it's Father Yule you're off to meet. He sits up there on the treeless summit, except when he's in a ravine. You'll definitely know him when you get near…"

Gusty stopped to crunch on icy lichens and watched Otto in silence. He wondered if this little man might be a touch stupid, especially with such a small head.

"Nice to meet you," Otto stammered, surprised at the flood of chatter. "Thank you very much for the advice. I'll follow that path up the mountain, unless you can recommend a faster route?"

The herd kept chewing and staring at Otto. His tiny legs amused them, but his friendly eyes and courteous manners made them smile approvingly.

"I can guide you," Gusty answered at last. "We'll be moving to the northern ravine soon anyway."

Gusty studied Otto's legs and went on, "You can't stride through the snow with legs that short. Hop on my back and we can chat on the way."

Otto gratefully accepted the offer. He left his skis on the side of the mountain and clambered onto Gusty's back. Gusty bellowed a signal and the herd set off. The reindeer moved leisurely together until they were all following, like furry waves over the blue snow.

While Gusty chattered, Otto sang softly to himself to stay calm; he was nervous and excited at the prospect of finally meeting Father Yule:

Here in the fells,
Past the Ironworm cruel,
The reindeer take me
Towards Father Yule.

When the herd finally reached the foot of the huge mountain, Gusty stopped and looked up. "You can continue on your own from here," he told Otto. "We don't go high into the mountains at night. But it isn't far now – especially if the old man is sitting on the summit. Then again, he may be somewhere else…"

Otto climbed down from Gusty's back and thanked the reindeer profusely.

Gusty mumbled a reply as he bent down to nuzzle for lichen in the snow. Otto could still hear him mumbling to himself as he turned towards the mountain.

The bare slope rose gently, but its summit loomed far in the distance. Otto listened to the silence of the frozen night, broken only by the squeak of his footsteps in the snow.

The North Star shone brightly above. Despite being far from home and on his own, Otto suddenly felt light and happy – even though he hadn't yet found what he was searching for. As he smiled to himself, he heard a beautiful voice singing, and stopped to listen.

The song grew louder. It rang over the mountain slopes and seeped into every valley. Never before had he heard anything like it. He moved towards the magical music.

It was hard climbing in the dark against the biting wind. But the voice made Otto forget the cold and climb faster. The song gave him energy.

Now Otto could make out the glimmer of a campfire. Beside the fire a large grey figure was singing an ageless chant of the north, making the mountains tremble.

14. Fires in the Sky

Otto approached the crackling fire. Sparks flew into the sky and the smell of smoke floated in the air. The light blinded him until his eyes adjusted.

The singer wound down his song and looked at Otto standing beside the fire in awe. A grey-white beard covered the face of a tall, robust old man. Lively dark eyes studied Otto from under thick eyebrows. The old man wore a long grey overcoat, woollen mittens and thick, laced boots. On his head was a leather hat adorned with large horns.

The old man spoke in a low voice, gesturing beside him. "Have a seat, my friend," he said.

Otto took a seat on a log covered with a fur rug. He gazed in enchantment at the old man.

"You've travelled a long way," said the old man as he stoked the fire. "Have some tea to warm and revive you."

Otto accepted the wooden cup that was held out to him. It steamed with fragrant crowberry tea, which filled him with such warmth he heaved a sigh.

"Are you Father Yule?" he asked hesitantly.

The old man laughed kindly. "I have been called that. You, little Otto, have been seeking me a long time, it seems. I hope I'll be able to help you." Noticing Otto's surprise, he winked and explained, "The lonttis were quite right to call themselves my secret spies. Now tell me: what can I do for you?"

Otto dug the battered postcard he had found on the beach out of his pocket. "I've been looking for Christmas,

for a light in the dark winter," he sighed. "But I haven't found any light that can banish the darkness."

The old man rubbed his thick beard and looked at the traveller. "How has your journey been?" he asked.

Otto told him about the wonderful creatures he'd met, the stories he'd heard and the many traditions he'd encountered on his travels. With a smile, he concluded, "I've learned that you have to prepare for Christmas and that it's a festival celebrated in midwinter. But I haven't seen any light that drives away darkness."

"That is exactly what you've seen," the old man said quietly.

Otto was confused.

"Friends gather together to share food and company and create bright memories – all these things brighten the darkness of winter. You have already experienced Christmas."

Otto was stunned. He had expected to find a physical object – a ball that shone as brightly as ten lanterns. Now he didn't know what to think.

The old man picked up a carved wooden staff. He tapped it, sending tiny silver sparks soaring into the sky.

"Each of those sparks represents someone you met on your journey. Each gleams brightly on its own..."

He tapped the staff again. This time the sparks wove together into a beautiful glowing design.

"But together these sparks shine much more brilliantly," he continued. "Each has a small piece of the story to tell, a small ray of light to contribute – but you already know that."

Now Otto understood. He had lived adventures, heard stories and shared happy times with many nice creatures.

Christmas was all these things combined, and that had created light in the winter's dark. No huge lantern was needed, just friendship.

"So what do you have to do with Christmas?" Otto finally asked.

With a smile, the old man tapped his staff on the frozen ground. The pattern in the sky compressed into a brightly flashing ball that dropped into his hand. He extended it to Otto and said, "I'm just here to remind you all."

The light dimmed, and Otto could now see a small drum where the ball had been. He took it and gazed at it, mesmerised. In it he saw pictures of the sea and of trees, and at its very centre was a seagull. Otto's heart filled with joy as he remembered his good friend Schooner.

The old man leaned against his staff and looked at Otto. With sparkling eyes, he said gently, "But we can also enjoy another kind of light at the heart of winter."

Otto had no time to reply before the old man began a new chant, which sped across the snows like a magic symphony and spurred the fire's sparks into a dance. The music was still echoing over the mountain fells when the old man suddenly disappeared.

Otto sat beside the fire feeling confused. He relived his journey, and realised that everything he had experienced would remain forever in his heart. The light generated through friendship would keep shining even if the roof of his hut collapsed. Even if he were flattened to the size of a mouse dropping. He thought again of Seagull Schooner and Little Grump, who would be worrying and waiting for him at home.

A red fox padded out of the darkness. It sat down beside Otto, fluffing its bushy tail and looking at him with yellow eyes.

"The old man has arranged a swift return home for you," the fox said, "but the fires of winter have yet to be lit. Would you care to accompany me for the ceremony of light?"

"I would love to," Otto agreed, intrigued by the fox's eloquent invitation.

The fox brushed snow on the fire to put it out and led Otto to the edge of a steep slope. It looked thoughtfully at the sky. Otto watched as the fox began to leap about, whisking snow with its tail until it swirled and whirled and illuminated the dark with remarkable colours.

The colours twirled high and spun in great circles up to the stars, where they transformed into flames of ever more astonishing hues. The heavens blazed with waves of brilliant green that turned now flame red, now golden yellow.

Otto watched, captivated. Clutching the drum to his chest, he felt light flooding through him.

The fox padded over to sit beside him and together they watched in awe as the lights danced across the heavens.

When the flares finally faded, Otto could see the sun peeking from behind the mountain – the bright line along the horizon, a promise of spring.

Otto had reached the end of his journey.

The fox swished its tail in farewell as Otto climbed onto the back of an enormous snowy owl and took off, speeding towards home.

Little Grump was sitting in the dim hut watching through the window as the sun sank into the sea. The edge of the water still crackled with thin ice, but the waves in the distance foretold the coming of spring. A loud swishing sound outside startled him from his daydream.

A moment later Otto stepped through the door to greet him. He burst right into stories about his journey and showed Little Grump his handsome drum.

Little Grump listened absently to Otto's tales without showing any hint of enthusiasm, but secretly he was relieved to have his old friend back. He thought the trip sounded dull and the light of winter a real let-down – much less exciting than a handsome new storm lantern. But seeing Otto's shining eyes gave him an idea.

Word soon reached Seagull Schooner that his old friend had returned safely, and the next day he swooped down towards the hut on the rocky shore.

"Greetings, old friend!" Schooner called out.

"Greetings!" Otto replied warmly. "How good it is to see you again! Do you want to hear about my journey?"

The following year, on the darkest night, just when Otto and Schooner were lighting the lanterns, Little Grump placed two packages wrapped in silver paper on the kitchen table. They contained pies he had baked himself from the very sweetest blueberries, saved especially for his friends.

Back in his cubbyhole he grumbled to himself about how dreadfully good giving these gifts made him feel.